JUST SO STORIES

JUST SO STORIES

RUDYARD KIPLING

Om KIDZ
An imprint of Om Books International

First published in 2020

Om KIDZ | Om Books International

Corporate & Editorial Office
A-12, Sector 64, Noida 201 301
Uttar Pradesh, India
Phone: +91 120 477 4100
Email: editorial@ombooks.com
Website: www.ombooksinternational.com

Sales Office
107, Ansari Road, Darya Ganj,
New Delhi 110 002, India
Phone: +91 11 4000 9000
Email: sales@ombooks.com

Retold by Swayam Ganguly

ISBN: 978-93-5376-560-6

Printed in India

10 9 8 7 6 5 4 3 2 1

Contents

Chapter One

How the Whale Got His Throat

Once upon a time, in the wide open sea, there lived a Whale. He ate the starfish to the garfish, the crab to the dab, and the plaice and the dace. He ate the skate and his mate, the wonderful mackerel and the pickereel, and the twirly-whirly eel. Slowly, all the fishes in the sea disappeared in the belly of the whale, till only one small fish remained. This one was a small 'Stute Fish, and he swam just a little behind the Whale's right ear, to be completely out of harm's way, and away from the mouth of the whale.

The Whale did not have any more fish to eat, and was very hungry. "I am so hungry!" the Whale stood up on his tail and declared, although there were no more fish left in the sea to hear him. But the small 'Stute Fish heard him loud and clear.

"Oh noble and generous Catacean," the small 'Stute fish addressed the Whale in his small s'tute voice. "Have you ever tasted Man?"

"No!" the Whale boomed. "What does it taste like?"

"Well, it's rather nice," the small 'Stute fish replied. "Man is nice to taste, although a little nubbly."

"Fetch me some then," the Whale ordered, impatiently thrashing the sea repeatedly with his tail, and making it froth up.

"No, no," the small 'Stute fish protested. "You don't need many. One at a time is quite enough. If you swim to latitude Fifty North, longitude Forty West, you will discover, sitting on a raft,

right in the middle of the sea, with nothing on his body but a pair of blue canvas breeches and a pair of suspenders (you must not forget the suspenders). I am talking about a shipwrecked Mariner who is armed with only a jackknife, but he is a man of immeasurable means and intelligence."

So, the Whale swam and swam to latitude Fifty North, longitude Forty West. When he reached, there on a raft, in the middle of the sea, clad only in a pair of blue canvas breeches and a pair of suspenders (you must particularly remember the suspenders, Best Beloved) and armed with only a jackknife, he discovered a solitary shipwrecked Mariner.

Then, the Whale opened his mouth so wide that it almost touched his tail! The mouth went back, and further back, and the shipwrecked Mariner went straight into the Whale's mouth. He was swallowed along with his raft, his blue canvas breeches, his suspenders (which

you must never forget), and his jackknife. The Whale swallowed them all straight down into his warm, dark, inside cupboards, and smacked his lips contentedly.

But just as the Mariner, a man of immeasurable means and intelligence, had reached well inside the Whale's warm, dark, inside cupboards, he jumped and stumped, bumped and thumped, danced and pranced, banged and clanged, bit and hit, creeped and leaped, howled as he prowled, jumped and pumped, hopped and dropped, cried and sighed, bawled as he crawled, and stepped and he lepped. The Whale was not very happy at the Mariner's antics. "This man is very nublly, indeed," he complained to the 'Stute Fish. "Also, he is making me hiccough. What should I do?"

"Why don't you ask him to come out?" the 'Stute Fish suggested.

"You come out and behave yourself now!" the

Whale shouted down his own throat to the shipwrecked Mariner in his tummy. "Thanks to you, I've got the hiccoughs."

"No!" the Mariner refused. "I shall think about coming out only when you take me to my natal-shore and the whitecliffs-of- Albion."

Then, the Mariner started jumping and dancing once again, only more vigorously, causing the Whale much discomfort.

"You better do as he asks, and take him home immediately," the 'Stute Fish advised. "This Mariner is a man of immeasurable means and intelligence."

So, the Whale swam as hard as he could to reach the natal-shore and the white-cliffs-of-Albion, where the Mariner's home was. The Whale rushed halfway up the beach as soon as he reached it, and opened his mouth wide. "Change here for Ashuelot, Winchester, Keene, Nashua, and other stations on the Fitchburg Road," the Whale announced. As soon as the word 'Fitch'

had escaped his mouth, the Mariner walked out. Now, the Mariner was a man of immeasurable means and intelligence. While he was in the Whale's stomach, and not jumping and dancing about, he had kept himself busy. He had cut up his raft into a small square grating with his jackknife. This square grating ran all criss-cross, and he had tied it firmly with the help of his suspenders. (Now you know why you were not supposed to forget the suspenders!)

After this, he dragged the grating nicely and tightly right into the throat of the Whale. It stuck there! Then, the Mariner recited this following *Shloka:*

By means of a grating
I have stopped your ating.

After this adventure, the Mariner stayed home, got married, and lived happily ever after. So did the Whale, but because of the grating in his throat, he could not cough up or swallow down. This prevented him from eating anything

in the sea except very, very small fish. That my dear boys and girls, is the reason why whales nowadays never eat men, women, boys or girls. As for the small 'Stute Fish, he went and hid himself in the mud under the Door-sills of the Equator, because he was scared that the Whale might be angry with him. The Mariner took the jackknife home, and was wearing the same blue canvas breeches when he stepped out on the shingle. The suspenders were discarded by him as they had to be used to tie the grating securely. That, my friends, is the end of that tale! Now, you know How the Whale Got His Throat!

Chapter Two

How the Camel Got His Hump

When the world first began, it was not so new-and-all, and a Camel lived bang in the middle of a Howling Desert. This Camel was an excruciatingly idle creature. Whenever anyone spoke to the Camel, the only answer received was 'Humph!' and nothing more. One day, the Horse came cantering to the Camel on a Monday morning, with a saddle on his back, and chewing a blade of grass. "O Camel, come out of this desert and trot like the rest of us," he invited. "Humph!" the Camel replied, and the Horse trotted away to tell the Man. Then, the Dog arrived, with a stick in his mouth. "O Camel, why don't you come and fetch and carry like the rest of us?" he stated.

"Humph!" the Camel declared, and the Dog ran away to tell the Man. Then, the Ox arrived with a yoke harnessed on his neck. "O Camel!" he declared. "Come and plough just like the rest of us."

"Humph!" the Camel replied, and the Ox went away to tell the Man.

When the day ended, the Man assembled the Horse and the Dog and the Ox, and addressed them, "It's obvious that Humph-thing in the Desert is incapable of work. If he could work, surely he would have arrived here by now. So, what I am going to do is leave him alone, but you Three must work double-time so that his absence is made up for."

The Three were very angry, as they thought

that this was an unfair decision. So, they held a palaver, an indaba, and a punchayet as well as a pow-wow right on the edge of the Howling Desert. What happened next was unimaginable! That Camel came rolling towards them, chewing milkweed most excruciating idle, and laughed at the Three. Imagine that! Then, he said 'Humph!' and left.

The Three had not yet recovered from their rage when the Djinn in charge of All Deserts arrived. He made a special appearance, rolling into view in a cloud of dust (Well, to be honest, Djinns always travel that way and it is special because it is Magic). This one was a busy Djinn indeed, but he took a break to stop and palaver and pow-wow with the Three.

"O Djinn of All Deserts," the Horse addressed him. "Do you think anyone has the right to sit idle, especially with the world being so new-and-all?"

"Definitely not," the Djinn replied.

"Well, I think you should know that a thing that lives bang in the middle of your Howling Desert (oh he's a Howler himself), having a long neck and long legs, refuses to do even a bit of work since Monday morning. He just won't trot!"

"Wow!" the Djinn exclaimed, whistling. "I daresay that's my Camel, for all the gold in Arabia! What does he have to say?"

"Well, all that he says is 'Humph'," the Dog replied.

"Doesn't he say anything else?" the Djinn demanded.

"Only 'Humph'. That's all! He just won't plough."

"That's very good!" the Djinn stated. "Now I'll humph him if you kindly wait."

The Djinn raised up a dust storm, and rolled himself in his new dust-cloak. Then, he flew across the desert where the Camel was

idly parked beside a pool of water, staring at his own reflection sadly.

"Ah, my long and bubbling friend," the Djinn stated. "What is this I hear about you? It seems that you do not do any work, what with the world being so new-and all!"

"Humph!" the Camel replied. The Djinn sat down, holding his chin in his hand, conjuring up a Great Magic, while the Camel stared at his own reflection in the water.

"The Three have been burdened with extra work ever since Monday morning, thanks to your excruciating idleness," the Djinn said to the Camel.

"Humph!" the Camel responded.

"I wouldn't say that again if I were you," the Djinn stated. "The reason is you might say it once too often. Bubbles, get this straight. I want you to work!"

"Humph!" was all the Camel said again. But

no sooner had he said that, he saw his back, a back that he was so very proud of, puffing up into a massive lolloping humph.

"Do you see that?" the Djinn stated. "Now that's your very own humph. You've brought it upon your own self by refusing to work. You've done no work at all since Monday, when the work actually began, and today is Thursday! But now you have to work, Bubbles!"

"But how can I work with this humph on my back?" the Camel protested.

"That's been made because you missed three days of work. Now, you shall be able to work for three whole days without eating, because you will be able to survive thanks to your humph. Now, step out of the Desert, and go to the Three and behave. Humph yourself!"

So, the Camel humphed himself, and he went, humph and all, to join the other Three. From that day onwards, the Camel can always

be seen wearing a humph (well, we call it a 'hump' now, so that his feelings are not hurt in any way); but the truth is that the Camel has never quite caught up with the three days of work that he missed when the world was just beginning. Till date, he has also never learned how to behave properly.

Chapter Three

How the Rhinoceros Got His Skin

A Parsee lived on an uninhabited island on the shores of the Red Sea. The rays of the sun reflected from his splendid hat in a way more than just Oriental. This Parsee lived with only his hat, knife, and cooking-stove. One day, the Parsee made a giant cake with flour, water, plum, currants, sugar and other stuff. But just as he was about to eat his cake, something arrived on the beach from the Altogether Uninhabited Interior of the island. It was a Rhinoceros with two piggy eyes, a horn on his nose, and very

little manners. Back in those days, the skin of the rhinoceros was the perfect fit for him, without any wrinkles whatsoever.

The Rhinoceros didn't have any manners then, and doesn't have any manners now. Come to think of it, an animal like the Rhinoceros will never have any manners! The Parsee instantly abandoned his cake, and climbed to the top of a palm tree. The Rhinoceros upset the oil-stove, using his nose, and the cake fell with a thud on the sand. Spiking up the cake with the horn of his nose, the Rhinoceros devoured it. Then he left, and the Parsee climbed down from the tree. He recited the following, rare *Sloka.*

Them that takes cakes
Which the Parsee-man bakes
Makes dreadful mistakes.

Now, let me tell you that there was a great deal more in that *Sloka* than you think. This is because, just five weeks later, the Red Sea

experienced a great heatwave. The Parsee took off his hat, but the Rhinoceros took off his entire skin. It was so hot that when the Rhinoceros came down to the beach to have his bath, he carried his skin over his shoulder. Those days, Rhinoceros skins could be buttoned underneath, with the help of three buttons, and resembled a waterproof. He waddled straight into the water blowing bubbles through his nose. But he made one fatal mistake! He left behind his skin on the beach!

The Parsee discovered the skin, and smiled a smile that ran all over his face not once, but twice. Then, he danced thrice around the skin and rubbed his hands in glee. He went to his camp immediately, and filled his hat with cake-crumbs, as the Parsee never ate anything but cake, you see, and so he had lots of cake-crumbs. Neither did the Parsee ever sweep out his camp. The Parsee took the skin,

and shook the skin. He scrubbed and rubbed the skin, ensuring that the skin was full of old, dry, stale, tickly cake-crumbs and a few burned currants. Then, he left it lying where it was, climbed to the top of his palm tree and waited. The Rhinoceros finished his bath and emerged from the water. He put on his skin, buttoning it up with the three buttons. The cake-crumbs started tickling, and as he scratched, things went from bad to worse. The Rhinoceros lay down on the sand, and rolled to make the tickling go away. But the tickling only got worse.

The Rhinoceros dashed to the palm tree and rubbed himself against it. He rubbed himself so hard and so much that his skin was rubbed into a great fold over his shoulders. Another fold appeared underneath just where the buttons were, but he rubbed so hard that the buttons fell off. Then he rubbed his legs so that more folds appeared over them.

This spoiled the Rhinoceros's temper, but the cake-crumbs continued to be inside his skin, and they continued to tickle. So, the Rhinoceros went home, extremely angry and horribly itchy. From that day onwards, all the Rhinoceroses have great folds in their skins and a very bad temper indeed, thanks to the cake-crumbs inside their skin. After the Rhinoceros left, the Parsee alighted from the palm tree, wearing only his hat, which reflected the rays of the sun in more than oriental-splendour. He gathered his cooking-stove, and headed towards the direction of Orotavo, Amygdala, the Upland Meadows of Anantarivo, and the Marshes of Sonaput.

Chapter Four

How the Leopard Got His Spots

Once upon a time, the Leopard lived in an area called the High Veldt. This place was exclusively empty, hot, and shiny. Here, the sand was plentiful, there was sandy-coloured rock, and exclusive tufts of sandy-yellowish grass.

The Giraffe, the Zebra, the Eland, the Koodoo, and the Harteebest were the neighbours of the Leopard, and they were all exclusively sandy-yellow-brownish all over their body. But the Leopard was the exclusivest sandiest-yellowest-brownest

animal, exactly coloured like the exclusively yellowish-greyish-brownish colour of the High Veldt area to the last hair. Now, this was pretty bad for the other animals, as the Leopard would lie down beside a stone or a clump of grass that was exclusively yellowish-greyish-brownish, and when the other animals passed by, he would surprise them out of their wits.

The Leopard hunted with his teeth and claws, but there was another hunter in the High Veldt. He was an Ethiopian hunting with his bow and arrows. Caught between the two hunters, the Giraffe and the Eland and the Koodoo and the others did not know which way to jump, Best Beloved. They didn't have a clue!

After a long time, the other animals became conditioned to avoid anything that resembled a Leopard or an Ethiopian. Slowly, they left the High Veldt, and travelled for many days to reach

a great forest, full of trees and bushes, and patchy-blatchy shadows with stripes and speckles. They hid here, and after a long time, after standing half in the shade and half in the sun, the Giraffe grew blotchy, the Zebra became stripy, and the Eland and the Koodoo became darker. They had small wavy grey lines running on their backs like bark on a tree trunk. One could hear and smell them, but they were seldom visible. The Leopard and the Ethiopian were so hungry that they ate rats, beetles, and rock-rabbits, and suffered from severe tummy ache. Finally, they met Baviaan- the dog headed, barking Baboon, Quite the Wisest Animal in Entire South Africa. "Where has all the game gone?" the Leopard asked Baviaan. Baviaan just winked.

"Can you tell me the current habitat of the aboriginal Fauna?" the Ethiopian asked Baviaan. Now, that meant the same thing as the question posed by the Leopard, but the

Ethiopian always used long words as he was a grown-up. Baviaan winked and replied, "The game has left to seek other spots. O Leopard, seek out other spots as soon as you can."

"That's all right," the Ethiopian stated. "But I want to know where the aboriginal Fauna has migrated."

"The aboriginal Fauna has decided to join the aboriginal Flora as it was high time for a change," Baviaan replied. "O Ethiopian, I would advise you to change as fast as you can."

The Ethiopian and the Leopard were puzzled, and set forth to look for the aboriginal Flora. After many days, they arrived at a forest that was great, high, and tall. The tree trunks were speckled, sprottled and spottled, dotted and slashed and splashed, and hatched and cross-hatched with shadows. (Say that aloud quickly to realise how very shadowy the forest was)

"What is this place that is so exclusively dark, and yet has little pieces of light?" the Leopard asked.

"I have no idea," the Ethiopian confessed. "But it should be the aboriginal Flora. I can smell him, I can hear him, but I can't see Giraffe!"

"That's strange!" the Leopard replied. "I can hear Zebra, I can smell him, but I can't see him."

"Maybe it's because it's been a long time since we've hunted them, and forgotten how they look like," the Ethiopian suggested.

"Fiddle!" the Leopard exclaimed. "I remember them clearly, especially their marrowbones. Giraffe is almost seventeen feet high, and of golden-yellow colour. Zebra is approximately four and a half feet high, and coloured grey-fawn."

"Hmmm," the Ethiopian stated. "If that is the case, then they should be visible in this dark forest like ripe bananas in a smoke-house!"

But the animals were not visible, even though the two hunters searched for them all day. "Let's wait till dark," the tired Leopard suggested at teatime. When darkness descended, the Leopard heard the noise of something breathing. He jumped at the source of the noise, and came into contact with something that felt and smelt like Zebra. When he brought the animal down, it even kicked like Zebra. But the Leopard was still unable to see it!

"Be quiet, you formless person!" the Leopard declared. "I am going to sit on your head till dawn, as there's something about you that I cannot understand."

Suddenly, he heard a grunt, and then a crash, and a scramble.

"I've caught something, but I can't see it," the Ethiopian shouted. "It smells like Giraffe, and it even kicks like him. But it's formless!"

"Don't trust it," the Leopard warned. "Just sit on its head as I'm doing, and wait till dawn.

None of 'em have any forms."

So, the two hunters sat hard on the invisible heads till morning.

"What do you have at the end of your table, Brother?" the Leopard asked.

"Well, it ought to be Giraffe," the Ethiopian replied, scratching his head. "But it's got chestnut-blotches all over its body. What do you have at the end of your table, Brother?"

"Well, it ought to be Zebra," the Leopard replied. "But it's got black and purple stripes all over its body."

"What have you done to yourself, Zebra?" he demanded. "Why, I could spot you from ten miles away on the High Veldt. But now, you are formless!"

"Can't you see that this isn't the High Veldt," the Zebra replied.

"Well, I can now. But I couldn't all day yesterday. How does this happen?"

"Set us free, and we will show you," the Zebra demanded, and he was freed along with the Giraffe. Zebra moved away to some little thorn-bushes, where the sunlight descended all stripy, and Giraffe shifted to some tall trees where the shadows were all blotchy.

"Now watch!" they announced together. "This is the way it's done. One-two-three! Where's your breakfast now?"

Both the Leopard and the Ethiopian stared hard, but the Zebra and the Giraffe had disappeared completely! All they could see were stripy and blotched shadows in the forest.

"Wow!" the Ethiopian exclaimed in wonder. "Now, that's a trick worth learning, Leopard. You could turn up in this dark forest like a bar of soap in a coal mine."

"Ha! Ha!" the Leopard replied. "Well, you could show up here like a mustard-plaster on a sack of coals."

"Calling each other names won't fetch us dinner, surely," the Ethiopian stated. "The fact here is that we don't match our backgrounds. I'm taking Baviaan's advice and changing my skin."

"To what?" the Leopard stated excitedly. "A nice working blackish-brownish colour, with a purple patch upon it, and touches of slaty-blue maybe? Why, it will be perfect to hide in the hollows and behind trees."

The Ethiopian decided to change his skin then and there, and this further excited the Leopard, who had never seen a man change his skin before.

"What about me?" he enquired.

"You should take Baviaan's advice. He told you to go into spots."

"Well, I did just that. I went into other spots, just like this one with you. Look what good it did to me!"

"Baviaan didn't mean spots in South Africa," the Ethiopian explained. "He was referring to the spots on your skin."

"Hmm. I won't look like Zebra, that's for sure," the Leopard replied.

"You must decide, as I wouldn't like to go hunting without you. But I have to if you insist on resembling a sunflower against a tarred fence."

"I'll take spots then," the Leopard decided. "But don't make them vulgar-big spots as I would never like to look like Giraffe!"

"Stand still!" the Ethiopian ordered. "I'll make the spots with my fingertips that still have plenty of black left."

The Ethiopian put his five fingers close together, and pressed them hard on the Leopard's skin. Wherever they made contact, they left five small black marks, all close together. You can spot them on any Leopard's skin, Best Beloved.

spot them on any Leopard's skin, Best Beloved. Well, sometimes the Ethiopian's fingers slipped, and the marks got a bit blurred. But there are always five spots made by five fat fingertips.

"What a beauty you are now!" the Ethiopian exclaimed. "You shall resemble a heap of pebbles when you lie on the naked ground, a piece of pudding-stone on the bare rocks, a piece of sunshine through the dappled leaves, when you hang on a leafy branch, and when you lie on the middle of the road, you can look like nothing in particular. Just think of that and purr!"

"But why didn't you go spotty as well then?" the Leopard asked suspiciously.

"Ah, plain black is best for a Negro," the Ethiopian declared. "Now, rush along and let's see if we can get even with our breakfast."

So, they left, Best Beloved, and lived happily ever after!

Oh, yes, you will hear grown-ups say every now and then, "Can the Ethiopian change his skin? Can the Leopard change his spots?"

I don't think grown-ups would say such silly things if the Leopard and the Ethiopian hadn't attempted it once, do you? But, Best Beloved, let me assure you that they will never do it again, as they are very happy as they are now.

Chapter Five

The Elephant's Child

In the High and Far-Off Times, the Elephant was without a trunk. He only had a blackish nose that bulged. It was as big as a boot, and he could wiggle it from side to side. But he could not pick up things with it. However, there was one Elephant's Child who was consumed with curiosity. He asked too many questions about Africa, where he lived.

When he asked his tall aunt, the Ostrich, why her tailfeathers grew the way they did, she spanked him hard with her hard, hard claws. His tall uncle, the Giraffe spanked him hard

with his hard, hard hoof when he enquired what made his skin spotty. He was spanked by his broad aunt, the Hippopotamus, with her broad, broad paws, when he asked why her eyes were red, and by his hairy uncle, the Baboon, with his hairy paw, when he asked him why melons tasted the way they did. But still, the Elephant's Child kept asking questions and kept getting spanked!

One fine morning, the Elephant Child asked a fine, new question he had never asked before- "What does the crocodile have for dinner?"

"Hush!" everybody said loudly, and he was spanked for a long time continuously. After the spanking, he saw the Kolokolo Bird sitting on a wait-a-bit thorn bush, and said, "I want to know what the crocodile has for dinner."

"Well, go to the banks of the great grey-green, greasy Limpopo River, abundant with fever trees, and find out," the Kolokolo Bird replied,

with a mournful cry.

The next morning, the Elephant's Child armed himself with a hundred pounds of bananas (the little, short, red variety), and a hundred pounds of sugar-cane (the long, purple variety), and seventeen melons (the greenycrackly variety), and declared to his families, "Goodbye everyone! I am going to the Limpopo River to discover what the crocodile has for dinner."

They spanked him once again for luck, and he left, a little warmer, eating melons. He kept dropping the melon rinds as he travelled as he couldn't pick them up with his small nose. At last, he arrived at the banks of the Limpopo River, and it was just as the Kolokolo Bird had described it. He had never seen a Crocodile before in his life, and the first thing he encountered was a Bi-Coloured-Python-Rock-Snake, coiled around a rock.

"Excuse me," the Elephant's Child asked most politely. "Have you seen a Crocodile in these promiscuous parts?"

"Have I seen a Crocodile?" the Bi-Coloured-Python-Rock-Snake asked scornfully. "Whatever will you ask me next?"

"Could you tell me what the Crocodile has for dinner please?" the Elephant's Child enquired. The Snake quickly uncoiled himself from the rock, and spanked the Elephant's Child with his scalesome, flailsome tail.

The Elephant's Child politely bid goodbye to the Bi-Coloured-Python-Rock-Snake, and helped him coil up on the rock again. Then, he went his way. Suddenly, he trod on a log of wood at the very edge of the Limpopo River. But it was actually the Crocodile, who winked one eye- like this!

"Excuse me," the Elephant's Child asked most politely. "Have you seen a Crocodile in these promiscuous parts?"

The Crocodile winked the other eye now, and lifted his tail half out of the mud. The Elephant's Child stepped back quickly, as he did not wish to be spanked again.

"Come here, little one," the Crocodile urged. "Why do you ask such a thing?"

"Excuse me, but I can't do that," the Elephant's Child said. "I have been spanked by my parents, aunts and uncles, and most recently by the Bi-Coloured-Python-Rock-Snake who spanks harder than all of them. I really don't want to be spanked anymore."

"Come hither, Little One," the Crocodile urged again, "for I am the Crocodile!"

Then, he wept crocodile-tears to demonstrate that it was the truth!

Now, the Elephant's Child was so excited that he kneeled down on the sand, and exclaimed, "You are the very person I have

been in search of for so many days. Please tell me what you have for dinner?"

"Come closer, O Little One," the Crocodile said. "Let me whisper in your ear."

The Elephant's Child brought his head closer to the musky, tusky mouth of the Crocodile, who caught him by his nose instantly.

"I think I will begin my dinner with Elephant's Child today," the Crocodile declared between his teeth.

"Led go! You are hurting be!" the Elephant's Child spoke through his nose. The Bi-Coloured-Python-Rock-Snake arrived at this moment, and said to the Elephant's Child, "My young friend, if you do not, at this very moment, pull as hard as you can, it's my humble opinion that your acquaintance in that large-pattern leather ulster (he meant the Crocodile here) will jerk you into yonder limpid stream before you can say Jack Robinson."

By the way, this is the way Bi-Coloured-Python-Rock-Snakes always speak.

So, the Elephant's Child sat back on his little haunches, and pulled as hard as he possibly could. He pulled, and pulled, and pulled, and his nose began to elongate. The Crocodile struggled in the water, which turned creamy as the Crocodile's tail lashed on it. The Elephant's Child pulled harder, and with each pull, his nose became longer. The Crocodile was pulling him inside the water, and the Elephant's Child could finally feel his legs give away.

"This is too butch for me," the Elephant's Child said through his nose, which was almost five feet long now. The Bi-Coloured-Python-Rock-Snake came to the rescue, by knotting himself in a double clove-hitch around the Elephant Child's hind legs.

"O rash and inexperienced traveller, let us now dedicate ourselves to a little tension. If

we do not, I'm under the impression that our self-propelling man-of-war armed with the armour-plated upper deck (By this, he meant the Crocodile) will permanently exterminate your future career."

By the way, this is the way Bi-Coloured-Python-Rock-Snakes always speak.

So he pulled, and so did the Elephant's Child, and the Crocodile pulled too. But the first two pulled the hardest, and the Crocodile was forced to abandon the pulling battle. He let go of the Elephant's Child's nose, and the 'plop' sound that it made could be heard all the way up and down the Limpopo.

The Elephant's Child thanked his slithery friend. Then, he wrapped his poor nose in cool banana leaves, and hung it to cool in the great greygreen, greasy Limpopo. "Why are you doing that?" the Bi-Coloured-Python-Rock-Snake asked.

"My nose is badly out of shape. I have to wait for it to shrink," the Elephant's Child explained. "I'm afraid you have to wait for a long time then," the Bi-Coloured-Python-Rock-Snake replied. "Some people do not know when good happens to them."

The Elephant's Child waited for three long days for his nose to shrink. But it never did! You see, the Crocodile had pulled it to make it the trunk that all Elephants have today. At the end of the third day, a fly stung him on the shoulder. Before he knew what he was doing, the Elephant's Child swatted the fly dead with the end of his trunk.

"Vantage number one!" the Bi-Coloured-Python-Rock-Snake exclaimed. "Would you have been able to do that with a mere-smear nose? Try and eat now!"

The Elephant's Child scooped up a large bundle of grass with his trunk, dusted it clean against his forelegs, and shoved it into his mouth.

"Vantage number two!" the Bi-Coloured-Python-Rock-Snake exclaimed. "Could you have done it with a mere-smear nose? Now, isn't the sun really hot today?"

"Yes," the Elephant's Child said, and before he knew what he was doing, he had schlooped up a schloop of mud from the banks of the Limpopo, and slapped it on his head to cool down. It made a cool schloopy-sloshy mud-cap, trickling behind his ears.

"Vantage number three!" the Bi-Coloured-Python-Rock-Snake declared. "You couldn't have done that with a mere-smear nose, could you? Now, what are your thoughts on being spanked again?"

"Excuse me," the Elephant's Child replied. "But I wouldn't like it at all."

"Would you like to spank somebody?"

"I shall like that very much, indeed!"

"I think you will discover that your new nose shall be very helpful in that regard," the Bi-Coloured-Python-Rock-Snake declared.

"Thank you!" the Elephant's Child replied, and set off for home.

He travelled across Africa, whisking and frisking his trunk. He pulled down fruit from a tree whenever he needed it, instead of waiting for it to fall down as he did previously. He plucked grass up from the ground, instead of kneeling down and eating. He broke off a tree branch and used it as a weapon to keep the flies at bay when they attacked him. He made himself a cool mudcap when the sun was hot.

When the Elephant's Child was lonely, he sang songs down his trunk, and it was noisier than several brass bands. He found a broad Hippopotamus (no relation of his) and spanked her rather hard, to ensure that the Bi-Coloured-Python-Rock-Snake had spoken the truth about

his new trunk. He also picked up the melon rinds that he had dropped on his way, as he was a Tidy Pachyderm.

He arrived home one dark evening, and greeted his dear families, who were very glad to see him. He coiled up his trunk, and said, "How do you do?"

"Come here and be spanked for your satiable curiosity," they said.

"Pooh!" the Elephant's Child declared. "I think you people know nothing about spanking. But I do. Here! Let me demonstrate!"

Using his trunk, he knocked down two of his brothers immediately.

"Great bananas!" they exclaimed. "Now, where did you learn that trick? What happened to your nose?"

"The Crocodile on the banks of the great grey-green, greasy Limpopo River gave me a new one," the Elephant's Child replied. "I asked

him what he had for dinner, and he gave me a new nose."

"It looks rather ugly," his hairy uncle, the Baboon stated.

"But it's rather useful," he replied, and picked up the Baboon, by his hairy leg, and flung him into a hornet's nest. Then, that bad Elephant's Child spanked all his families one by one, till they were both warm and stunned. The tall aunt Ostrich's feathers were plucked, the Giraffe was dragged through a thorn bush, the broad Hippopotamus aunt was shouted at, and bubbles blown into her ear while she was taking a nap in the water after lunch. But the Elephant's Child never let anyone harm the Kolokolo Bird.

All his dear families decided to visit the Limpopo River to borrow new noses from the Crocodile there. When they returned, no one spanked anyone anymore. So, after that day,

O Best Beloved, all the Elephants that you will see, besides all that you won't, have trunks exactly like the trunk of the satiable Elephant's Child.

Chapter Six

The Sing-Song Of Old Man Kangaroo

The Kangaroo was not always as we see him now. He was a totally Different Animal, having four short legs. He was grey, wooly, and excessively proud. He danced on an outcrop in the middle of Australia, and worshipped the Little God Nqa. One day, he visited Nqa at six, before breakfast, and requested, "Make me different from all the animals by five this afternoon."

"Go away!" Nqa ordered angrily. Then, the Kangaroo visited the Middle God Nquing at

eight, after breakfast. "Make me different from all the other animals and also make me the most popular by five this afternoon!" he declared. "Go away!" Nquing ordered angrily. So, the Kangaroo visited the Big God Nqong at ten, before dinner. "Make me different from all the other animals and also make me the most popular by five this afternoon!" he pleaded.

Nqong jumped up from his bath in the salt-pan, and exclaimed, "Yes, I will!"

He called Dingo-Yellow-Dog Dingo, who was always hungry and dusty.

"Dingo! Do you see that gentleman dancing? He wants to be popular and run after. Make him so, Dingo!" Nqong ordered.

"That cat-rabbit?" Dingo enquired. Dingo-Yellow-Dog-Dingo, who was always hungry and grinning like a coal mine, ran after Kangaroo. The Kangaroo ran on his four little legs like a bunny. He ran through the desert,

the mountains, through the salt-pans and the reed-beds, through the blue gums and the spinifex. The Kangaroo ran till his legs ached. He had to, as Dingo chased him relentlessly.

Old Man Kangaroo ran through the trees, through the mulga and the grass; he ran through the Tropics of Capricorn and Cancer. Soon, they arrived at the Wollgong River. There was no bridge or ferry boat to cross over, and the Kangaroo stood on his legs and hopped! He had to! He hopped through the Flinders and the Cinders, and through the deserts in Central Australia. He hopped like a Kangaroo! Initially, he hopped one yard, then three yards, and then, five yards! His legs became stronger and longer, and he didn't even stop for the refreshment he badly wanted. He hopped like a cricket; like a pea in a hot saucepan; and a new rubber ball on the nursery floor. Tucking up his front legs, he used his hind legs to hop, sticking out his tail

behind him for a balance-weight as he hopped through the Darling Downs.

"It's five o' clock," Nqong announced suddenly.

Poor-Dog Dingo, always hungry and dusty, sat down. He hung out his tongue and howled. Old Man Kangaroo sat down, and said, "Thank God that's over!"

"You should thank Yellow-Dog Dingo for all that he's done for you," Nqong stated.

"He's chased me out of my childhood home; out of my regular meal-times; changed my shape that will never return; and played Old Scratch with my legs!" the Kangaroo protested.

"Didn't you ask me to make you different from the other animals, and sought after too?" Nqong stated.

"Yes, I wish that I hadn't now," the Kangaroo replied. "I thought you'd use charms and incantations, instead of a practical joke."

"Joke?" Nqong exclaimed, rising from his bath.

"Say that again and I'll have Dingo run your hind legs off!"

"I apologise!" the Kangaroo said. "Your Lordliness, I just wanted to state that I haven't had anything to eat since morning."

Dingo said the same thing, and Nqong asked them to come the next day. So, both were left in the middle of Australia, each blaming the other for the situation. "It's all your fault!" each said.

Chapter Seven

The Beginning of the Armadillos

In the middle of the High and Far-Off Times, there lived a Stickly-Prickly Hedgehog on the banks of the Amazon. His friend was the Slow-Solid Tortoise. There also lived a Painted Jaguar who ate frogs and beetles when he could not catch deer or monkeys; and when he could not hunt down frogs and beetles, he went to his Mother Jaguar for advice, who told him how to catch and eat tortoises and hedgehogs.

"My son," she said to him. "When you find a Hedgehog, you must drop him into the water and wait for him to uncoil. After catching a

Tortoise, you must scoop him out of his shell, using your paw."

One night on the banks of the Amazon, Painted Jaguar discovered Stickly-Prickly Hedgehog and Slow-Solid Tortoise seated together. They did not have time to flee, and so, Stickly-Prickly curled himself into a ball, and Slow-Solid retreated into his shell.

"My mother told me to drop a Hedgehog into the water so he would uncoil, and to scoop out a Tortoise from his shell. Now which one of you is a Tortoise and which one a Hedgehog? I can't tell to save my spots!" Painted Jaguar asked.

"Are you sure your Mummy told you that?" Stickly-Prickly Hedgehog asked. "Maybe she said that to uncoil a Tortoise, you need to shell him out of the water with a scoop, and when you paw a Hedgehog, you must drop him on the shell."

"Yes, are you quite sure your Mummy told you

that?" Slow-Solid Tortoise enquired. "Maybe she said that when you water a Hedgehog, you must drop him into your paw, and you must shell a Tortoise till he uncoils."

"No, no, I don't think she said that," a confused Painted Jaguar said. "But please say it clearly again."

"When you are scooping water with your paw, you uncoil it with a Hedgehog," Stickly-Prickly declared. "Now, remember that as it's important!"

"But when you paw your meat, you drop it into a Tortoise with a scoop," the Tortoise added.

"You two make my spots ache," Painted Jaguar said. "I didn't ask for your advice. I just wanted to know which of you is Tortoise, and which is Hedgehog?"

"I won't tell you," Stickly-Prickly stated. "You can scoop me out of my shell if you want."

"Ah, now I know you are Tortoise," Painted

Jaguar declared, and thrust out his paw just as Stickly-Prickly curled himself up into a ball. Jaguar's paw was filled with prickles, and he painfully knocked the Hedgehog away into the bushes of the woods. Painted Jaguar put his wounded paw into his mouth, and the prickles hurt him even more.

"Well, now I know that he wasn't a Tortoise after all," Painted Jaguar stated. "But how do I know that the other one is?"

"But I am Tortoise," Slow-and-Solid insisted. "Your mother was right when she told you to scoop me out of my shell with your paw. Start!"

"You said she said something different just a minute ago," Painted Jaguar said, sucking the prickles out of his paw.

"Well, if you say that I said she said something different, how does that make any difference?" Slow-and-Solid declared. "If she said what you said I said she said, isn't it the same as if I said what she said she said. But, if you think she told you to uncoil me with a scoop, instead of pawing me with a shell, how can I help that?"

"What will happen if I scoop you out of your shell?" Painted Jaguar asked suspiciously.

"I have no idea, as no one has ever done that. But if you want to see me swim away, all you have to do is drop me in the water."

"I don't believe you," the Jaguar replied. "You've mixed up everything my mother said. She said one of you must be dropped into the water. As you seem most anxious to be dropped, I think you really don't want to be dropped. So jump right in and be quick about it!"

Slow-and-Solid dived into the turbid Amazon, and swam to the bank where Stickly-Prickly waited for him.

"That was a rather narrow escape," Stickly-Prickly declared. "I don't like that Jaguar. What did you tell him?"

"I told him the truth, that I'm a Tortoise," Slow-and-Solid told Stickly-Prickly what had happened. "Now, he's gone off to tell Mummy!"

The two eavesdropped on the conversation between Painted Jaguar and his mother from behind the bushes.

"Son, I see prickles in your paddy-paw," Mother Jaguar exclaimed. "You must have encountered a Hedgehog. Why didn't you drop him into the water?"

Painted Jaguar told his mother what had happened. "These animals on the turbid Amazon are too clever for me. I think we should find lodgings elsewhere."

"Son, remember my advice! A Hedgehog curls himself into a ball and his prickles stick out!"

"I don't like this old lady at all," Stickly-Prickly stated. "Wonder what else she knows."

"However, a Tortoise can't curl himself up," Mother Jaguar continued. "He just tucks himself

up into his shell safely!"

"I don't like this old lady one bit," Slow-and-Solid Tortoise declared. "Why, even painted Jaguar won't forget those directions. What a pity you can't swim, Stickly-Prickly!"

"Just think how easier it would be if you could curl up," Stickly-Prickly retorted. Painted Jaguar, in the meanwhile, was sitting on the banks of the turbid Amazon, sucking prickles out of his paw and talking to himself-

'Can't curl, but can swim-
Slow-Solid, yes that's him!
Curls up, but can't swim-
Stickly-Prickly, yes that's him!

The Tortoise and the Hedgehog decided that the Hedgehog would learn how to swim, and that the Tortoise would learn how to curl up. After a great deal of practice, and helping each other, they were totally transformed.

"Scales are a great improvement over prickles,

and now I can swim," Stickly-Prickly exclaimed. "Let's go find Painted Jaguar and surprise him!"

Painted Jaguar was so stunned to see them that he fell thrice backwards over his own tail. The two curled themselves up, and rolled around Painted Jaguar repeatedly till his eyes did cartwheels in his head. He ran to fetch his mother.

"There are two new animals in the woods, mother," he declared. "The one you said can't swim, can, and the one you said couldn't curl up, can. Besides, both of them have got scales now from a smooth and a prickly skin. I don't feel comfy at all."

"Son, how many times do I have to tell you that a Hedgehog is a Hedgehog, and a Tortoise is a Tortoise!"

"But mother, it's a bit of both!"

"We'll call it 'Armadillo' till we find out its real name. It's best to leave them alone."

Painted Jaguar did as advised, but the strangest thing is that everybody on the banks of the turbid Amazon have called Stickly-Prickly and Slow--Solid 'Armadillo' from that day onwards. One can find Hedgehogs and Tortoises in other places, of course, my garden for example. But the real old and clever ones, with their pine-cone scales, and residing on the banks of the Amazon are always called Armadillos because they are so clever.

Chapter Eight

How the First Letter Was Written

Once upon a very early time, lived a Neolithic man. This man was a Primitive, living cavily and happily in a Cave, and wore scarce clothes. He couldn't read or write, and didn't want to. His name was Tegumai Bopsulai, meaning, 'Man-who-does-not-put-his-foot-forward-in-a-hurry '; but we shall call him Tegumai.

His wife's name was Teshumai Tewindrow, meaning, 'Lady-who-asks-a-very-many-questions'; but we shall call her Teshumai. Their daughter's name was Taffimai Metallumai,

meaning, 'Small-person-without-any-manners-who-ought-to-be-spanked'; but we shall call her Taffy. But she was her parents' Best Beloved, and she was not spanked half as much as she ought to have been, and the three were a happy family. As soon as Taffy could run, she accompanied her Daddy everywhere. Now pay attention!

One day, Tegumai went down through the beaver-swamp to the Wagai River with Taffy, to spear carp-fish for dinner. Tegumai's spear was a wooden one with shark's teeth at the end. By accident, he broke it before he started fishing. The two were many miles away from home, and although they were carrying their lunch in a little bag, Tegumai wasn't carrying extra spears.

"It'll take me half the day to mend this spear," Tegumai exclaimed.

"Let me run back to the Cave, and fetch your

big black spear," Taffy offered, but Tegumai refused as she was too small to run so far, and she could be drowned. So, he started repairing the spear.

"Daddy, it's such a shame that we don't know how to write. We could have sent a message home for a new spear otherwise," Taffy observed.

Suddenly a stranger appeared. He belonged to a far tribe called the Tewaras, and did not understand Tegumai's language. When he saw Taffy, he was reminded of his own little daughter, and so he stood on the bank and smiled at her. Tegumai continued mending his spear.

"Do you know where my Mummy lives?" Taffy asked the stranger.

"Um!" he replied, not understanding a word.

"Silly!" Taffy responded, by stamping her foot. This was because she had spotted a shoal of big

carp go upriver just when her Daddy couldn't use his spear.

"Don't disturb grown-ups," Tegumai said busily mending his spear, not even bothering to turn around.

"I'm not," Taffy replied. "I just want him to do what I want, and he doesn't understand."

"Don't disturb me then," Tegumai stated.

The stranger sat down on the grass, and Taffy showed him what her Daddy was doing. *What a wonderful child she is!* the stranger thought. "She makes faces at me and stamps her foot. She must be the daughter of that great noble chief who doesn't pay any heed to me."

"I want you to go to my Mummy, as you have longer legs than me and because you won't fall into the beaver-swamp," Taffy declared. "Ask for Daddy's other spear- the spear with the black handle that hangs over our fireplace."

This is a very wonderful child! the stranger

thought. "She waves her arms and shouts, but I don't understand a word she says. But if I don't do her bidding, I'm afraid that vain Chief, who turns his back to me, will be very angry indeed."

He got up and got a big flat piece of bark from a birch tree to hand it over to Taffy. He did this to demonstrate that his heart was as pure as the birch-bark, and that he did not mean no harm. But Taffy did not understand, and thought he wanted her Mummy's address. "I can't write, but I can draw pictures with something sharp," she stated. "Lend me the shark's tooth from your necklace!"

The stranger did not reply, and Taffy pulled at the stranger's beautiful bead and seed and shark-tooth necklace that adorned his neck.

She's a very wonderful child indeed! the stranger thought. *This is a magic shark's tooth, and anyone else touching it without my permission would have instantly swelled up and burst. But this child did not, and that Big Chief still hasn't taken any notice of me. He also doesn't seem afraid about his child. I have to be more polite.*

He handed Taffy the shark's tooth, and first, she drew her Daddy fishing.

"I've drawn his broken spear, so Mummy will know. Now, I'll draw his black-handled spear," she declared. "Now, it looks as if it's sticking into Daddy's back, but that's because the shark's tooth slipped while I was drawing, and as this piece of bark is small. What I'll do is draw a picture of myself explaining this to you also. My hair is only standing up because it's easier to draw. Now, I'll draw you, and put the spear that Daddy wants in your hand in my drawing. But I can't make you as pretty as you are. Please don't be offended!"

The stranger smiled. He thought that a big battle was going to be fought somewhere seeing Taffy's drawings, and that Taffy wanted him to

fetch the Great Chief's tribe.

"Stop when you come to these two trees here in my drawing." Taffy said. "Then, you cross this hill till you come to this beaver-swamp. I can't draw beavers so I'm not putting them. But I'm drawing their heads as that's all you'll see of them while crossing the swamp. Be careful not to fall in! Our Cave lies just beyond the beaver-swamp. That's my Mummy outside. She is the most beautifulest Mummy that ever was. Show the picture to her and she'll give you the spear! I've drawn her holding up her hands as I know she's going to be happy to see you. Isn't it a beautiful picture? Do you want me to explain again?"

The stranger looked at the picture and nodded vigorously.

I understand, he thought. *If I don't fetch the Great Chief's tribe to help him, he will be slain by his enemies advancing from all sides. Now I know why*

he was pretending not to notice me as his enemies hiding in the bushes would see him passing a message to me. So, the wise man let his wonderful child deliver the message instead. I must get help for him.

The stranger ran like the wind with the birch-bark in his hand, and Taffy sat down, pleased with herself. Now, this is the picture that Taffy had drawn!

The stranger ran for a few miles, and discovered Teshumai at the door of her Cave, by sheer accident. She was talking with a few Neolithic ladies, and as Taffy resembled her mother, the stranger recognised her easily. He smiled politely, and handed her the birch-bark. He had run hard, his legs were scratched by brambles, and he was panting. But he was still polite!

Teshumai screamed like a Banshee and flew at the stranger after seeing the picture.

The Neolithic ladies knocked him down and sat on him, making a long line of six as Teshumai yanked at his hair.

"Look!" she displayed the picture to the Neolithic ladies perched patiently on the stranger. "He has stuck spears into my Tegumai, and scared Taffy so much that her hair stands on end. He has the cheek to bring me a picture of it. Here is my Tegumai with his arm broken, surrounded by men with spears. A whole bunch of people (they were beavers really) are coming from behind him. Shocking, isn't it?"

"Most shocking!" the Neolithic ladies exclaimed in unison, and the stranger was surprised when they filled his hair with mud. Then, they beat upon the Reverberating Tribal Drums to fetch the chiefs of the Tribe of Tegumai, with their Hetmans and Dolmans, Neguses, Woons, Akhoonds, Warlocks, Angekoks, Juju-men, Bonzes and others. They decided that the

stranger should lead them where he had hidden Taffy, before his head was chopped off.

The stranger was angry at this reception. But he led everyone to the bank of the Wagai River, where they saw Taffy making daisy-chains, and Tegumai spearing fish with his mended spear.

"Well, you came quickly!" Taffy exclaimed. "But why did you bring so many people? What a surprise, eh Daddy?"

"Indeed!" Tegumai replied. "But it has spoiled my fishing for the day. The entire Tribe is here, Taffy!"

So they were! Teshima and the Neolithic ladies walked in, holding the stranger. Behind them were the Head Chief, the Vice-Chief, the Deputy and Assistant Chiefs, the Hetmans and Heads of Hundreds, Platoffs with Platoons, Dolmans with Detachments, Woons, Neguses, and Akhoonds. All of them were armed to the teeth, and the Tribe followed them, shouting so much that they frightened the fish for twenty miles. Teshumai hugged and kissed Taffy, while the Head Chief of the Tribe of Tegumai shook Tegumai severely. "Explain! Explain! Explain!" the entire Tribe cried in unison.

"Let go of me!" Tegumai exclaimed. "Can't a man break his carp-spear without the whole countryside descending on him? How interfering!"

"You haven't got Daddy's spear too!" Taffy stated. "What are you doing to my nice stranger-man?"

The stranger was being whacked and thumped as he pointed at Taffy helplessly. "Where are the bad men who speared you, my darling?" Teshumai asked.

"There was no one," Tegumai replied. "The only visitor I had is the man you are trying to kill! O Tribe of Tegumai, are you well or ill?"

"He arrived with a terrible picture of you being speared," the Head Chief explained. "I gave him that picture," Taffy stated meekly.

"You?" The Tribe exclaimed together. "Small-person-with-no-manners-who- ought-to-be-spanked! You?"

"Explain! Explain! Explain!" the Head Chief exclaimed, hopping on one foot.

"Well, I drawed Daddy's spear as I wanted the stranger-man to fetch it," Taffy explained. "There wasn't many spears, and only one. But I drawed it thrice to make sure he understood. There was little space on the birch-bark so the spear stuck into Daddy's head. What Mummy called bad people were actually my beavers. I drawed them to show him the directions to the swamp. He is a nice stranger-man and you all are the stupidest people in the world. Why have you filled his hair with mud? Wash him right now!"

Everybody was silent for a long time, and then, the Head Chief laughed. The stranger laughed. Tegumai laughed so hard he fell down on the ground! The Tribe laughed louder and harder. The only ones not to laugh were Teshumai and the Neolithic ladies. "I didn't mean to," Taffy said. "I just wanted Daddy's blackhandled spear."

"Never mind," the Head Chief stated. "It's a great invention, and one day men will call it writing. Right now, it's only pictures, and as today has demonstrated, pictures can be misunderstood. But there will come a time, O babe of Tegumai, when we shall create letters, all twenty-six of them. Then, we shall be able to read and write, and say precisely what we want to express without making mistakes."

He ordered the Neolithic ladies to wash the mud off the stranger's hair.

"That would make me very happy," Taffy

stated. "That's because every other spear in the Tribe of Tegumai has been fetched, except my father's black-handled one."

"Well, next time you write a picture-letter, make sure you send someone who can speak our language as well," the Head Chief declared.

The stranger-man was adopted into the Tribe of Tegumai, because he was a gentleman and did not throw tantrums about the mud that had been put in his hair. From that day onwards, (I think it's Taffy's fault), very few little girls have liked to learn how to read and write. Most prefer to draw pictures and play with Daddy, just like Taffy.

Chapter Nine

How the Alphabet Was Made

A week after the earlier story ended, Taffy went carp-fishing with her Daddy again. "Daddy, I've thinked of a nice surprise. Make a sound! Any sound," Taffy said.

"Ah!" Tegumai said. "Will that do?"

"Yes. You look just like a carp-fish with its mouth open. Do it again!"

"Ah! Ah! Ah!" Tegumai said.

"Do it again Daddy, and keep your mouth open. I'm going to draw a wide open carp-fish's mouth with your tooth."

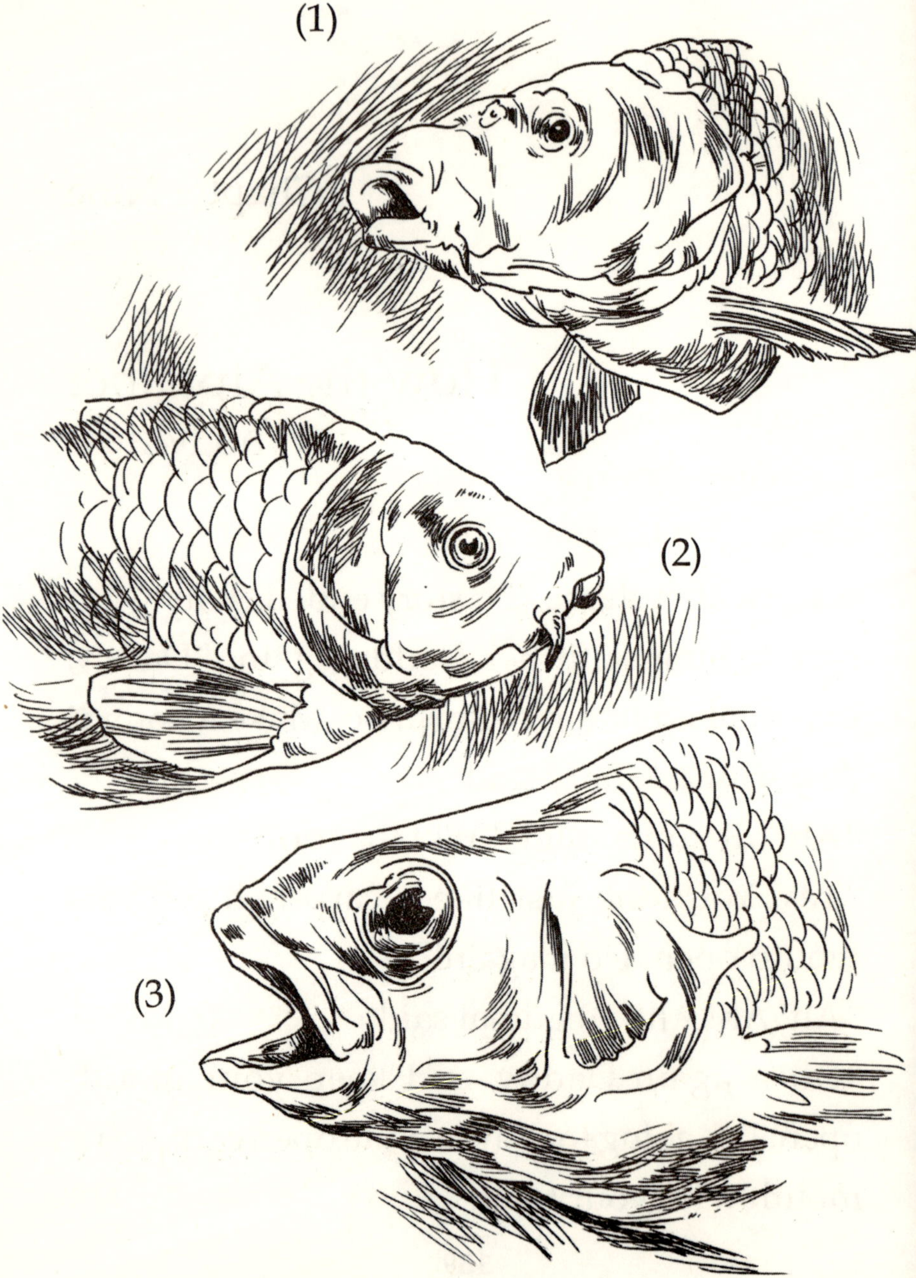
(1)
(2)
(3)

"What for?"

"It'll be our secret surprise," Taffy revealed. "I'll draw an open-mouthed carp-fish at the back of our cave, and it will remind you of your ah-noise."

Then, Taffy drew this. (1)

"Not bad!" Tegumai said. "But you've forgotten the feeler that hangs across his mouth."

"But, I can't draw, Daddy!" Taffy stated.

"You don't need to draw anything but the opening of his mouth, and the feeler across it," Tegumai explained. "Then, he'll look like a carp-fish as perches and trouts don't have feelers. See!" And, Tegumai drew this. (2)

"I'll copy it now. Do you understand this?" Taffy said, and drew this. (3)

Tegumai praised Taffy, who was very proud.

"Make another noise," she demanded.

"Yah!" Tegumai said loudly.

"That's a mixy noise," Taffy declared. "The

(4)

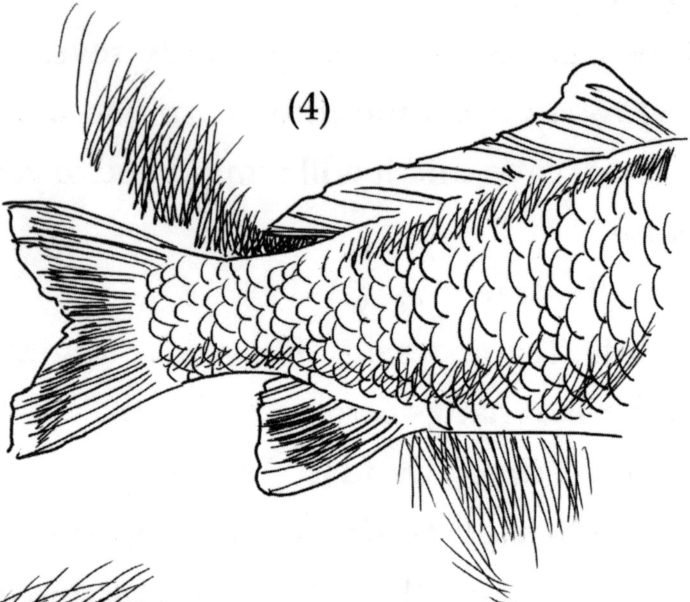

(5)

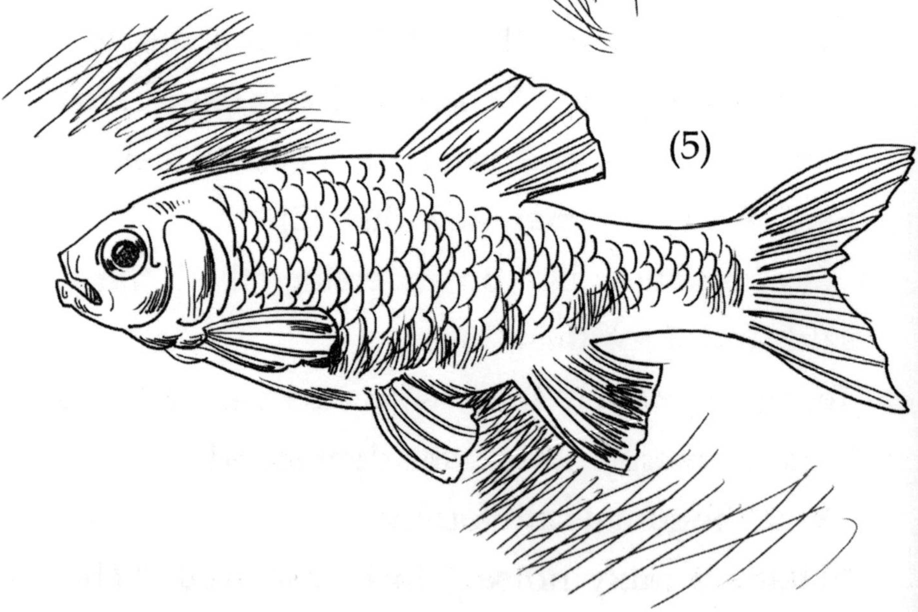

end part is ah-carp-fish-mouth. But what can be done about the front part? Yer-yer-yer and ah! Ya!"

"It's similar to the carp-fish mouth noise," Tegumai stated. "Let's draw another carp-fish and join them."

"No, I'll forget if they are joined," Taffy said. "Draw it separately. Draw his tail, as if he's standing on his head."

"Here's a carp-fish tail for the yer noise," Tegumai said, and drew this. (4)

"I'll try now," Taffy said. "But remember that I can't draw like you. So. I'll just draw the split part of the tail, and the sticky-down line for where it joins." She drew this. (5)

"Make another noise now, Daddy," Taffy urged.

"Oh!" Tegumai said loudly.

"That's easy!" Taffy stated. "Your mouth becomes as round as an egg or a stone. So that shape will do for that!"

(6)
(7)

Tegumai drew this. (6)

"Goodness gracious!" Taffy exclaimed. "What a lot of noise-pictures we've drawn! Make another noise, Daddy!"

"Ssh!" Tegumai said, and frowned, but Taffy did not notice.

"That's easy," she said, scratching on her bark.

"Eh, what?" Tegumai asked. "What I meant was that I was thinking, and did not want to be disturbed."

"It's a noise all the same, Daddy. It's the kind a snake makes when it doesn't want to be disturbed." And, she drew this. (7)

"When you draw a hissy-snake by the door of your little back cave, I'll know you're thinking hard, and I'll come in as quiet as a mouse. If you draw it on the tree by the river, I'll know you want me to be as quiet as a mouse while you're fishing."

"Very true," Tegumai replied. "I think you

(8)

have made the biggest invention ever since the Tribe of Tegumai started using shark's teeth as replacement for flints for their spearheads. I think we've discovered the big secret of the world."

Taffy was curious, and her Daddy explained.

"What's water in the Tegumai language?" he asked.

"Ya, and it means river as well- like Wagai-ya- the Wagai river."

"What is bad water like black or swamp-water that gives you fever if you drink it?"

"Yo."

"What if you saw this drawn by the side of the pool in the beaver-swamp?" Tegumai asked, and drew this. (8)

"Carp-tail and round egg. A mixture of two noises!" Taffy exclaimed. "I wouldn't drink that water as you said it was bad."

"If Yo is bad water, so is food cooked on the

(9)

(10)

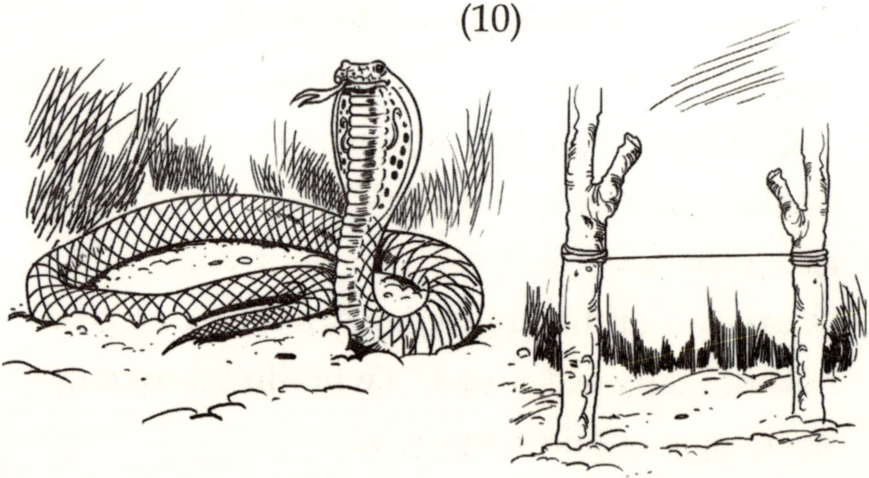

fire," Tegumai continued, and drew this. (9)

"Snake and egg," Taffy exclaimed. "That means dinner's ready! If one saw that scratched on a tree, one would know it was time to return to the Cave."

"But there is a problem here," Tegumai declared. "So means 'come and have dinner', but sho means the drying-poles where we hang our hides."

"Nasty old drying poles!" Taffy exclaimed. "What do we do now?"

"We must make a new picture for sho, a spotty snake that hisses sh-sh. The plain snake will only his ssss."

"I'm not sure how to put in the spots," Taffy confessed. "If one is in a hurry, one might forget to put them, and it would appear to be so when it is sho. It's better to draw them nasty drying-poles just after the hissy-snake."

And, Taffy drew this. (10)

(11)

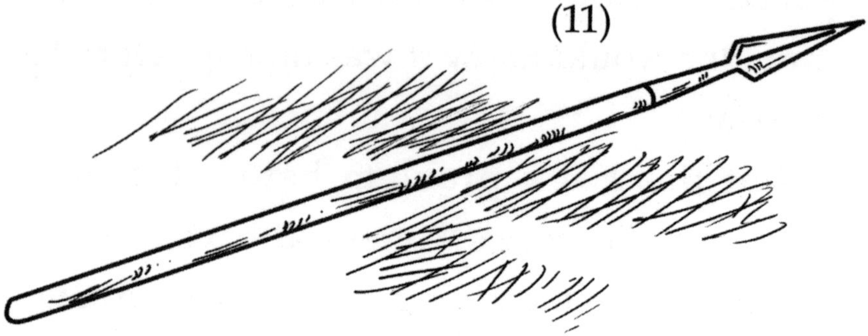

(12)

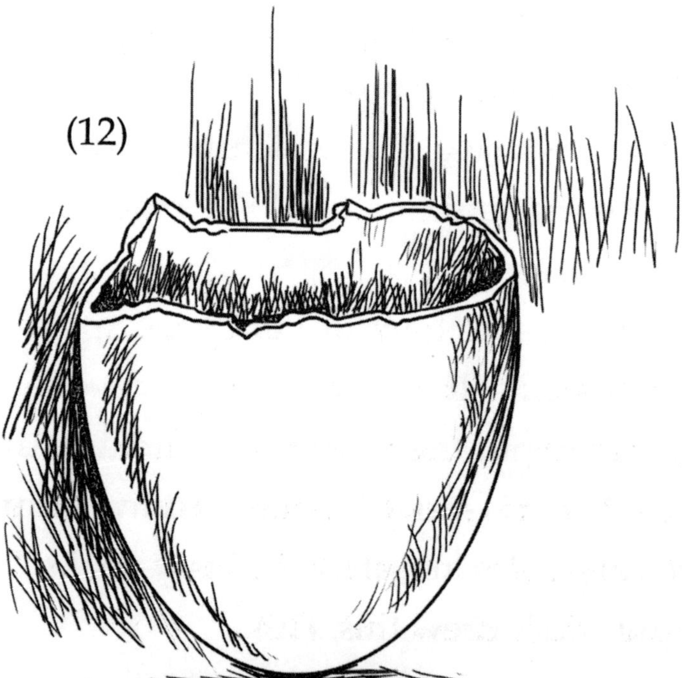

"That's safest," Tegumai laughed. "Now, I'll make a new sound- shi! That's Tegumai for spear!"

And, he drew this. (11)

"Now, we'll say shu, meaning sky," Tegumai declared. "We'll open a small hole at the end of the round egg to demonstrate the O-noise running thin, OOO-OO-OO, just like this!" And, he drew this! (12)

"Shu-ya means sky-water, or rain," Taffy exclaimed as a drop of water landed on her hand. "It's raining Daddy!" she stated. "Is that what you wanted to tell me?"

"Yes," Tegumai said. "I did so without speaking a word."

Taffy stood up and danced, and Tegumai joined his daughter. "What if I wanted to tell you that it wouldn't rain a lot, and that you should come down to the river, what would

I draw? Say the words for Tegumai first," he demanded.

"Shu-ya-las, ya maru. (Sky-water ending. Come to river.)" Taffy stated. "Many new sounds. How can we draw all of them?"

Tegumai exclaimed, "Wait a minute, Taffy, and we won't do any more today. We've done shu-ya already. But this las is a teaser! La-la-la!"

"The hissy-snake is at the end, and the carpmouth before the snake," Taffy stated. "All we need is la-la."

"Yes, we have to make la-la, and we're the first in the world to try," Tegumai declared.

"Las means breaking, finishing, or ending doesn't it?" a tired Taffy yawned.

"Yes," Tegumai replied. "Ya-las means no water in the tank for Mummy to cook with."

"Shi-las means your spear is broken," Taffy said. "If only I had thought that earlier when I was writing that picture-letter! After drawing shi,

(13)

(14)

(15)

(16)

I'd have drawn your broken spear this way!"
She drew. (13)
"That's perfect," Tegumai said. "That's la."
"Now for maru. Mum-mum-mum. Mum shut's one's mouth up, right? So, we'll draw a shut mouth." He drew. (14)
"Then the open carp-mouth. That makes Ma-mama! What about the rrrr- thing, Taffy?"
"It sounds rough and edgy, like your shark-tooth saw you use to cut out a plank to make your canoe," Taffy observed.
"You mean like this?" Tegumai said, and drew. (15)
"We don't want so many teeth," Taffy said.
"I'll put only one," Tegumai said, and drew. (16)
"There!" Tegumai declared. "They're all done. I'll draw them in a string just like fish."
"Shu-ya-las ya-maru," Taffy read aloud.

They decided it was enough for one day, and went home. The next day, they worked

(17)

(18)

(19)

on the sound-pictures again, and they became easier and simpler. The hissysnake was turned the other way round to produce the Z-sound, to show it hissing backwards softly and gently. (17) A twiddle was made for E, as it was a common alphabet. (18)

The picture of the sacred Beaver of the Tegumais was worked upon to produce the B-sound. (19) In this way, slowly and steadily they drew all the sound-pictures, and the Alphabets were all complete.

After thousands and thousands of years, after Hieroglyphics, Demotics, Nilotics, Cryptics, Cufics, Runics, Dorics, Ionics, and all other ricks and tricks, the Alphabets returned to their proper shape for all Best Beloveds to learn when old enough. But I remember Tegumai, Taffy and Teshumai, and all the years that flew by, a long time ago on the banks of the big Wagai!

The first thing Tegumai did after he and Taffy had created the Alphabet was to make a magic Alphabet-necklace of all the letters that was kept at the Temple of Tegumai forever. It took five years to get the necklace in order.

Chapter Ten

The Crab that Played With the Sea

At the Time of the Very Beginnings, the Eldest Magician first got the Earth ready, and then the Sea. Then, he told all the Animals, "You can come out and play now!"

Man arrived with his own little daughter sitting on his shoulder in the evening, and enquired, "What is this play, Eldest Magician?" "Son of Adam," the Eldest Magician replied. "This is the play of the Very Beginning; but you are too wise for this play."

"But see that all the Animals are obedient to me," the Man replied.

Pau Amma the Crab moved away as the two were speaking, to step into the sea. "I shall play my play alone in the deep waters," he pledged. "I will not obey this son of Adam!" Only the daughter of the Man saw Pau Amma leave. The play continued till all the Animals were briefed. Then, the Eldest Magician walked the world to see how the Animals were playing. He headed North, where he discovered the Elephant digging with his tusks and stamping on the brand new earth created for him.

"Kun?" the Elephant enquired, meaning, "Is this right?"

"Payah kun," the Eldest Magician replied, meaning, "Quite right!"

Then, he breathed on the rocks and great lumps of earth that the Elephant had thrown up. They were transformed into the Himalayan

Mountains, and you can look for them on the map.

Going East, the Eldest Magician found the Cow feeding in the field that had been prepared for her. She was licking at a whole forest with her tongue, and swallowed it.

"Kun?" the Cow asked.

"Payah kun," the Eldest Magician replied. Then, he breathed upon the empty patch where the Cow had eaten, and on the spot where she had sat down. The first became the Great Indian Desert, and the second, The Desert of Sahara, and you can find them in the map.

The Eldest Magician found the Beaver as he went West. The Beaver was making a beaver-dam across the mouths of rivers created for him.

"Kun?" the Beaver asked.

"Payah kun," the Eldest Magician declared. Then, he breathed upon the still water and the fallen trees, and they became the Everglades in Florida, and you may look for them in the

map. He went South after that to see the Turtle scratching the sand made for him with his flippers. The sand and rock whizzed in the air to land in the sea.

"Kun?" the Beaver asked.

"Payah kun," the Eldest Magician said. Then, he breathed upon the sand and the rocks that had fallen into the sea, and they became the outstandingly beautiful islands of Borneo, Celebes, Java, Sumatra, and the other islands of the Malay Archipelago. You can find them on the map!

One day, the Eldest Magician met the Man on the banks of the Perak River. "Son of Adam! Do all the Animals obey you?" he asked.

"Yes," the Man replied.

"Does all the Sea obey you?"

"No! Once a day, and once a night, the Sea overflows the Perak River and chases the sweetwater back into the forest. My house is

wet and full of mud, my canoe is upset. Did you ask it to play this play?"

"No," the Eldest Magician replied. "This is a new and bad play."

Just then, the great Sea showed itself at the mouth of the Perak River. It drove the river backwards, and flowed over the dark forests for miles to flood the Man's home.

"This is wrong play," the Eldest Magician stated. "Launch your canoe so we find out who is playing with the Sea."

They stepped into the canoe, and the Man's daughter accompanied them. The Man carried his kris, or curved dagger and they entered the river. The Sea sucked the canoe right in and they went past Selangor, Malacca, Singapore, right to the island of Bintang, as if pulled by a string.

"Beasts, Birds, and Fishes!" the Eldest Magician stood up and shouted. "Which one among you is playing with the Sea?"

"O Eldest Magician," they replied. "We play the games you have taught us. So do our children. None of us plays with the Sea."

The Moon rose just then, and the Eldest Magician spoke to the hunchbacked old man sitting on the Moon spinning a fishing line with the hope to catch the world one day, "O Fisher of the Moon, are you playing with the Sea?"

"No!" said the Fisherman. Then, the Eldest Magician asked the same question to the Rat up in the Moon who always bit the Fisherman's line. The Rat had the same reply.

"O Eldest Magician," the Man's little daughter exclaimed. "When you spoke to my father at the Very Beginning, and you were teaching the beasts their plays, one naughty beast entered the sea before you taught him his play."

"How wise little children are!" The Eldest Magician exclaimed. "They see everything and are silent. Describe this beast, child."

"Well, he was round and flat, and his eyes grew upon stalks," the girl replied. "He walked sideways and a strong armour covered his back."

"How wise little children are who are truthful," the Eldest Magician stated. "I know now where Pau Amma went."

He took the paddle, and they arrived at Pusat Tasek- the Heart of the Sea. There lies the great hollow that leads down to the heart of the world, Pauh Janggi, the Wonderful Tree, bearer of the magic twin-nuts. The Eldest Magician slid his arm through the water to touch the back of Pau Amma, the Crab, under the roots of the Wonderful Tree. The Sea rose up as water rises in a basin when you put your arm in it.

"Now I know who's been playing with the Sea," the Eldest Magician exclaimed. "Pau Amma! What are you doing?"

"Once a day, and once a night, I go out in search of my food," Pau Amma replied. "Leave me alone!"

"When you exit your cave, the waters of the Sea flood into Pusat Tasek, leaving the beaches of all islands bare, and killing the small fish. The legs of Raja Moyang Kaban, the King of the Elephants, are made muddy. When you return to sit in Pusat Tasek, the Sea rises and drowns half the small islands. Man's house is flooded, and Raja Abdullah, the King of the Crocodiles tastes salt water."

"Who would have thought that I was so important?" Pau Amma laughed. "From now, I shall go out seven times a day, and the waters will never be still."

"I cannot make you play the play you were supposed to play as you escaped me at the Very Beginning," the Eldest Magician declared. "But come up if you are not afraid, and we shall talk about it!"

"I'm not afraid," Pau Amma declared, and rose to the surface of the sea in the moonlight. Pau

Amma was the biggest thing in the world as he was the King Crab of all Crabs, and not just a common Crab. He was so huge that one side of his massive shell touched at Pahang beach, and the other at Sarawak beach. He was taller than the combined smoke of three volcanoes.

As Pau Amma rose, one of the great magical twin-fruits was uprooted. This was one of the magic double-kernelled nuts that make people young. It bobbled beside the canoe, and the little girl pulled it in. With her small scissors, she began to pick out its soft eyes.

"Make a magic to show how important you are, Pau Amma!" the Eldest Magician stated. Pau Amma tried to do so, rolling his eyes and waving his legs, but could only stir up the Sea. This was because he was only a Crab.

"You are not that important, after all, Pau Amma," the Eldest Magician laughed. "Let me try now!" he said, making a Magic with his left hand. Lo and Behold! Pau Amma's hard, blue-green-black shell fell off his body and he was left all soft. He was now as soft as the small crabs we find on the beach.

"Shall I ask Man to cut you with his kris?" the Eldest Magician demanded. "Shall I summon the King of the Elephants to pierce you with his tusks? Or should I ask the King of the Crocodiles to bite you?"

"I am ashamed," Pau Amma confessed. "Please return my shell to me. I shall return to Pusat Tasek, venturing outside only twice a day for food."

"No, I shall not," the Eldest Magician replied. "That will only make you stronger, prouder and bigger. You might forget your promise and play with the Sea again!"

Pau Amma lamented, saying that he would be eaten or die. So, the Eldest Magician assured him that the Seas would always be safe for him

and his children forever.

"But if not for Man, I might not have run away," Pau Amma stated. "What will Man do for me?"

"I will make a Magic so that both the deep water and the dry ground serve as a home for you and your children. You will be able to hide both on land and sea," Man declared.

"What about the girl there who saw me running away but never called me back?" Pau Amma demanded. "If she had spoken then, the Eldest Magician would have called me back, and none of this would have happened. What will she do for me?"

"This nut that I'm eating is a good one," the little girl replied. "I shall make a Magic and give you my pair of sharp, strong golden scissors. With its help, you and your children can eat coconuts all day long when you come to land from the Sea. You can also dig a shelter for yourself when there's no hole or stone nearby.

If the earth is hard, you can also climb a tree using these scissors."

"But as I'm still soft, these gifts won't help me," Pau Amma stated. "Return my shell, O Eldest Magician, and I will play your play."

"I shall return it for eleven months of the year, Pau Amma," the Eldest Magician replied. "But it shall grow soft again on the twelfth month of every year. This will be to remind you and all your children that I'm still capable of making Magics, and to keep you humble. You will become bolder once you can run both on land and water. Also, if you can climb trees, crack nuts, and dig holes, it will only make you greedier."

"I shall take all the gifts," Pau Amma declared, after some thought.

The Eldest Magician made a Magic with his right hand, and lo and behold, Best Beloved, Pau Amma began shrinking in size till he was

a small green crab swimming beside the canoe, whimpering, "Give me the scissors!" The girl picked up Pau Amma on her palm, seated him in the bottom of the canoe, and gave him the scissors. With his little arms, he waved them, opened, shut and snapped them, declaring, "I can eat nuts, crack shells, dig holes and climb trees. I can breathe in the dry air, and can find safety under every stone. I didn't know I was so important. Kun? (Is this right?)"

"Payah Kun," the Eldest Magician said, and laughed, and gave him his blessing. Little Pau Amma jumped into the water from the side of the canoe.

"Wasn't that done well?" the Eldest Magician asked, and the Man agreed. "But we must return to Perak now, and it's tiring to paddle for so long. If only we had waited till Pau Amma had got out of Pusat Tasek and come home, the water would have carried us there," the Man stated.

"As you are lazy, so shall your children be lazy," the Eldest Magician stated. "In fact, they shall be the laziest people in the world, and be called the Malazy, or lazy people."

Then, the Eldest Magician pointed to the Moon, and stated, "O Fisherman, see the Man too lazy to row home. Pull his canoe with your line!"

"No!" the Man exclaimed. "Let the Sea do my work for me twice a day forever if I have to be lazy. That way I won't have to paddle."

"Payah kun," the Eldest Magician laughed, and said.

So, the Rat of the Moon stopped biting the line, and the Fisherman let his line down till it touched the Sea. Then, the Fisherman pulled the entire deep Sea along, past Bintang, Singapore, Malacca and Selangor. Then, the canoe burst into the mouth of the Perak River again. The Eldest Magician instructed the Fisherman of the Moon to pull the Sea twice a day and twice

a night for ever, so that the Malazy fishermen did not have to paddle.

"But make sure you do not pull too hard, or I shall use Magic to punish you like I punished Pau Amma," the Eldest Magician warned.

From that day onwards, the Moon has always pulled the Sea up and down, creating what we call the tides. Sometimes, the Fisherman of the Moon does pull a bit too hard though, and what we get are spring tides. When he pulls softly, we get neap tides. But then again, he is always careful because of the Eldest Magician's warning.

When you visit the beach, you can see how Pau Amma's babies make small Pusat Taseks for themselves, under each stone and bunch of weed on the sands. You can spot them waving their little scisssors, and run up to land to eat coconuts in some parts of the world. But once every year, all Pau Ammas must shake off

DO
NOT HUNT
CRABS

their hard shells and be soft, as a reminder of the Eldest Magician's Magic. But just because Pau Amma was silly and rude a long long time ago, it isn't fair to hunt down or kill Pau Amma's babies today. Oh Yes! Let me tell you that Pau Amma's babies also hate to be taken away from their small Pusat Taseks, and kept in pickle-bottles at home. This is why they nip you with their scissors, and it serves you right!

Chapter Eleven

The Cat that Walked by Himself

Once upon a time, the Tame Animals were all wild, and walked in the Wet Wild Woods. But the wildest of them all was Cat, who walked by himself. Man was wild too, and got tamed only after he met Woman. Instead of a heap of wet leaves, she chose a nice dry Cave to sleep in, and she lay clean sand on the floor. She also lit a nice fire of wood at the back of the Cave, hung a dried wild-horse skin, tail first, across the door of the Cave. "Wipe your feet when you enter, dear," she said. "Now, we'll keep house."

That night, they feasted on wild sheep roasted on hot stones, flavoured with wild garlic and wild pepper; and wild duck stuffed with wild rice, wild fenugreek and wild coriander; and marrowbones of wild oxen; and wild grenadillas and wild cherries. Man slept beside the fire happily, although Woman sat up, combing her hair. She took the bone of the shoulder of mutton- the big flat blade-bone, threw more wood into the fire, and made a Magic- the First Singing Magic in the world!

In the Wet Wild Woods, Wild Dog smelled the roast mutton with his wild nose, and declared, "I shall go and investigate as I think it's good. Cat, come along!"

"Nenni!" Cat said. "I am the Cat who walks alone. I shall not come!"

Wild Dog went alone, and Cat followed him, remaining out of sight.

Woman saw him and laughed. "Here comes the

first Wild Thing from the Wild Woods! What do you want?"

"My enemy and the wife of my enemy, what is it that smells so good?" Wild Dog enquired.

"Taste and try," Woman said, throwing a roasted-mutton bone at Wild Dog. It was the most delicious thing he had ever tasted, and he begged for another.

"Help my Man hunt during the day, and guard our Cave at night," Woman stated. "I shall give you as many bones you want."

"Ah!" Cat said, listening. " Wise Woman! But she's not as wise as I am."

Wild Dog crawled towards Woman, and laid his head on her lap, agreeing to her conditions.

"Foolish Dog!" Cat stated, returning to the Wet Wild Woods, but not telling anybody. When Man woke up, Woman told him that Wild Dog was now their First Friend forever.

"Take him when you go hunting!" she ordered. The next night, Woman cut fresh grass from the water-meadows, and dried it before the fire. It smelled like newly mown hay. Then, she plaited a halter out of horse-hide. She looked at the shoulder-of-mutton-bone and made a Magic- the Second Singing Magic in the world.

In the Wild Woods, when Wild Dog didn't return, Wild Horse decided to go in search of him. Cat followed him.

"Here comes the second Wild Thing out of the Wild Woods," Woman said. "What do you want?"

"My enemy and the wife of my enemy, where is Wild Dog?" Wild Horse enquired.

"You did not come here for Wild Dog," Woman laughed. "You came here for this good grass!" Wild Horse begged for the grass, and Woman said, "Bend your head, and wear what I give you. You shall have this grass thrice a day!"

"Ah!" Cat said, listening. "Wise Woman! But she's not as wise as I am."

Woman slipped the plaited-hide halter over the wild head of Wild Horse as he bent down, agreeing to be her servant.

"Foolish Horse!" Cat stated, returning to the Wet Wild Woods, but not telling anybody.

"This is not Wild Horse anymore," Woman said to Man. "His name is First Servant, as he will carry us from one place to another forever. Ride him when you go hunting!"

The next day, Wild Cow arrived at the Cave, followed by Cat. The same thing happened, and Cow agreed to give milk to Woman in exchange of grass. Cat left again, but did not tell anyone. No other wild animal went to the Cave the next day. So, Cat went there himself and smelled the warm white milk.

"My enemy and the wife of my enemy, where is Wild Cow?" Cat asked Woman, who laughed and asked him to return to the woods, as they did not need any more friends or servants.

"I'm neither a friend nor a servant," Cat stated. "I am the Cat who walks alone, and I wish to enter your Cave."

"Then go away and walk by yourself," Woman said.

"Must I never enter the Cave?" Cat asked, pretending to be sorry. "Must I never sit by the fire and drink the warm white milk? You are so wise and beautiful! How can you be so cruel to a Cat?"

"Well, I knew I was wise. But I didn't know that I was beautiful," Woman said. "I shall make a bargain with you. You may enter the Cave whenever if I say one word in your praise. You may sit by the fire forever if I say two words in your praise, and if I say three words

in your praise, you may drink the warm white milk forever."

"Let the Curtain at the mouth of the Cave, the Fire at the back, and the Milk-pots beside the fire, remember what my Enemy and the Wife of my Enemy has said," Cat stated, and left.

Woman did not tell Man and Horse and Dog about the bargain made with Cat. Cat left and hid himself in the Wet Wild Woods for a long time till Woman completely forgot about him. Only Bat that hung upside down in the Cave was aware of Cat's hiding place. Every night Bat would fly to Cat and give him the news of the Cave.

"There's a Baby in the Cave now," Bat informed Cat one night. "He's new, pink, small and fat. Woman is very fond of him."

"What is the Baby fond of?" Cat asked.

"He likes soft things that tickle," Bat replied. "He loves warm things that he can hold in his

arms when he goes to sleep and also likes being played with."

"Ah! My time has come," Cat stated.

The next night, Cat crept closer to the Cave and hid next to it till morning. Man, Dog and Horse went hunting, and Woman was busy cooking. As Baby cried and disturbed her, she left him outside the Cave with some pebbles to play with. Cat stepped forward and patted Baby on the cheek with his paddy paw. Baby cooed. Then, Cat rubbed against Baby's fat knees, and tickled his fat chin with his tail. Baby laughed, and Woman heard him and smiled. Bat informed her that a Wild Thing from the Wild Woods was playing with her Baby most beautifully.

"Bless that Wild Thing," Woman exclaimed. "I was busy today and he has done me a service."

The moment this was uttered, the dried horse-skin Curtain at the mouth of the Cave

fell down with a woosh! It remembered the bargain that Woman had made with Cat. When Woman arrived to pick it up, she saw Cat sitting comfortably inside the Cave.

"My enemy, Wife of my enemy, and Mother of Enemy," Cat stated. "As you have spoken a word in my praise, I can sit in your Cave forever. But I am still the Cat who walks alone, and all places are the same to me."

Woman was angry, and she began spinning. But Baby cried as Cat was not playing with it, and despite her best efforts, Woman could not quieten Baby. Cat advised Woman to take a strand of thread, tie it to her spindlewhorl and drag it along the floor. Woman did so, and Cat ran after the small clay spindle-whorl, patting it with his paws and rolling head over heels. He chased it, pretended to lose it and pounced on it again. Baby laughed loudly and ran after Cat. It frolicked all over the Cave till it was tired and

settled down to sleep holding Cat in its arms. Cat then purred him a lullaby, and Baby was soon fast asleep.

"That was wonderfully done," Woman exclaimed. "O Cat, you are clever indeed!"

The moment this was uttered, the smoke of the Fire at the back of the Cave remembered the bargain Woman had made with Cat, and descended from the roof- puff!

When the smoke cleared, lo and behold! - Cat was sitting comfortably beside the fire!

"As you have spoken two words in my praise, I can sit by the warm fire at the back of your Cave forever," Cat stated to Woman. "But I am still the Cat who walks alone, and all places are the same to me."

Woman angrily started making a Magic that would stop her from praising Cat for a third time. It was a Still Magic, and the Cave grew

so silent that a small wee-wee mouse crept out of a corner to run across the Cave.

"Is that little mouse a part of your Magic?" Cat enquired.

"Ouh! Chee!" Woman exclaimed, jumping up on the footstool in fear. "Not at all!"

"Ah! Then that mouse will do me no harm if I eat it?" Cat asked.

"No!" Woman exclaimed. "Eat it quickly and I shall be forever grateful to you!"

Cat did so instantly.

"A thousand thanks!" Woman declared. "Even the First Friend cannot catch little mice as quickly as you can! You must be very wise indeed!"

That very moment, the Milk-pot by the fire cracked into two- fffft!- as it recalled the bargain made with Cat. Woman jumped down from the footstool as Cat lapped up the warm, white milk that flowed from the broken pieces.

"As you have spoken three words in my praise, I can drink the warm, white milk thrice a day, forever. But I am still the Cat who walks alone, and all places are the same to me."

Then, Woman laughed, and offered Cat a bowl of warm, white milk to drink.

"O Cat," she said. "You are as clever as Man! But keep in mind that your bargain was not made with either Man or Dog. I am not responsible for what they do when they will return home."

That evening, when Woman told Man and Dog everything, Man said, "He hasn't made a bargain with me or Men after me!"

Then, he collected his two leather boots, stone axe (that makes three) and a piece of wood and a hatchet (that makes five in total) and placed them in a row.

"Now, we will make our bargain," he said to Cat. "I shall throw these five things at you if you

don't catch mice when you are in the Cave, and so shall all Men after me."

"Ah!" Woman exclaimed. "Cat is not as clever as my Man!"

"I shall catch mice when I'm in the Cave," Cat declared. "But I am still the Cat who walks alone, and all places are the same to me."

"For having said that, I'm going to throw my boots and my stone-axe (that makes three) at you whenever I see you," Man stated. "So shall all Men after me."

"He hasn't made a bargain with me or with Dogs after me," Dog declared, baring his fangs. "If you are not kind to Baby when you are in the Cave, I shall hunt you down and bite you! So shall all Dogs after me!"

"Ah!" Woman exclaimed. "Cat is not as clever as Dog!"

"I shall be kind to Baby when I'm in the Cave, provided he does not pull my tail too hard,"

Cat declared. "But I am still the Cat who walks alone, and all places are the same to me."

"For having said that, I shall chase you up a tree whenever I see you," Dog promised. "So shall all Dogs after me!"

The Man threw his boots and stone-axe (that makes three) at Cat, who ran out of the Cave. Dog chased him up a tree. From that day onwards, three out of five men will always throw things at a whenever they see him, and all will chase him up a tree. But Cat keeps his part of the bargain, as he kills mice and is kind to babies when he is in the house, provided they don't pull his tail too hard. But sometimes, when the moon is up at night, Cat walks alone, and all places are the same to him.

Chapter Twelve

The Butterfly that Stamped

This story is new and wonderful, and quite different from the others. This is the story of The Most Wise Sovereign Suleiman-bin-Daoud-Solomon, the Son of David. This is the story of the Butterfly that Stamped.

Now listen!

Suleiman-bin-Daoud was a wise man, understanding the language of the beasts, birds, fishes and insects. He also understood what the rocks and the trees said. His Head Queen, the most beautiful Queen Balkis, was almost as wise as he was.

Suleiman-bin-Daoud wore a magic ring on the third finger of his right hand. With a single turn of this ring, he could summon Djinns and Afrits from below the earth to do his bidding. When he turned it twice, Fairies descended from the skies to follow his orders, and when he turned it thrice, the great Angel Azrael of the Sword arrived in the guise of a water-carrier, and narrated to him the news of the three worlds- Above-Below-and-Here.

Yet, Suleiman-bin-Daoud was not a vain man. He rarely showed off, and was sorry when he did. Once, he decided to feed all the animals in the world in a single day. When the food was ready, an Animal emerged from the deep sea to devour all the food in three mouthfuls.

"Who are you?" a surprised Suleiman-bin-Daoud asked.

"O King, I'm the youngest of thirty thousand brothers, living at the bottom of the sea. When

we heard you are feeding all the animals in the world, my brothers sent me to enquire when dinner would be ready."

"But you have eaten all the dinner I prepared for all the animals in the world! Suleiman-bin-Daoud exclaimed.

"Do you really call that a dinner?" the Animal stated. "We eat twice as much between meals."

Suleiman-bin-Daoud realised he had given that dinner to show how great a king he was, and not because he wanted to be kind to animals. He was ashamed, and never showed off after that.

Now, the real part of my story begins. Suleiman-bin-Daoud married nine hundred and ninety-nine wives, other than the Most Beautiful Balkis. They all lived in a huge golden palace in the middle of a beautiful garden with fountains. Some of the wives were nice, and some were horrid. The horrid ones quarrelled

with the nice ones and made them horrid. Then, they all quarrelled with Suleiman-bin-Daoud, making it horrid for him. But Balkis the Most Beautiful never quarrelled with Suleiman-bin-Daoud, as she loved him deeply.

Suleiman-bin-Daoud could have summoned the Djinns and the Afrits by twisting his magic ring, and all his nine hundred and ninety-nine troublesome wives would have been transformed into white mules or pomegranate seeds with magic. But he didn't do that as it would be showing off. So, whenever they quarrelled, he chose to take a walk alone. One day, when he did so, he met Balkis the Most Beautiful among the orange trees, who was sad that her husband was worried. She comforted him, and he continued with his walk. Balkis hid behind the trees so that she could be near her husband.

Suddenly, Suleiman-bin-Daoud heard two butterflies quarrelling under a tree.

"How can you talk like this with me?" one said to the other. "Do you know that if I stamp my foot, all of Suleiman-bin-Daoud's palace, including this garden, would disappear immediately in a clap of thunder?"

Suleiman-bin-Daoud forgot his problems and laughed loudly. He called the Butterfly, who was scared to death. He flew to rest on Suleiman-bin-Daoud's hand, who whispered, "Don't you know that all of your stamping wouldn't bend even a blade of grass? Why did you lie to your wife then?"

"O King, you know how wives are like," the Butterfly replied. "One has to keep them in order in any way. She has been quarrelling with me since morning, and I said that to make her quiet."

"Hope it quiets her, little brother," Suleiman-bin-Daoud replied. "Now return to her."

The Butterfly flew back to his excited wife.

"Suleiman-bin-Daoud himself heard you!" she exclaimed.

"Of course, he did! I meant him to," the Butterfly replied.

"What did he say?" the impatient wife asked.

"Well, he asked me not to stamp, and I promised I won't!"

The wife was quiet now, but Suleiman-bin-Daoud laughed so hard that tears ran down his face.

Balkis the Most Beautiful had overheard everything, and smiled to herself.

"I can save my Lord from his evil Queens if I am wise enough," she thought, and asked the Butterfly's wife to come to her. She flew to Balkis's white hand, totally frightened.

"Little woman, do you believe what your husband said?" Balkis whispered.

"O lovely Queen, you know how men are like," the Butterfly's wife said. "They get angry over nothing, but we must humour them. If

it pleases my husband that he can make the King's palace disappear by stamping his foot, I don't really care. He'll forget everything tomorrow."

"Next time he boasts, call his bluff," Balkis said. "Ask him to stamp! He'll be ashamed of himself!"

The Butterfly's wife flew away to her husband, and they started quarrelling in five minutes. The Butterfly threatened to stamp his foot, and his wife dared him to do it.

"I don't want to break my promise," the Butterfly said.

"You can't bend a blade of grass by stamping," his wife mocked. "I dare you! Stamp!"

Suleiman-bin-Daoud heard everything and laughed hard. The Butterfly came flying at him for advice now.

"I can't do it! Now, she'll mock me for the rest of my life!" he said.

""No! she won't," Suleiman-bin-Daoud said, twisting his ring to summon four huge Djinns. He ordered them to make his palace and gardens disappear with a clap of thunder when the Butterfly stamped his foot, and bring them back when he stamped his foot again. Then, he told the Butterfly to go and stamp.

The Butterfly flew to his wife and stamped. The Djinns carried away the palace thousands of miles away with a thunderclap, and everything grew pitch-black.

"Oh! I'm so sorry!" the Butterfly's wife cried, as she flew about in the dark. "I promise I'll be good. Just bring the gardens back, my dear darling husband!"

The Butterfly was as frightened as his wife, and Suleiman-bin-Daoud laughed so hard, that he recovered his breath only minutes later, to ask the Butterfly, "O Great magician, please stamp again and bring back my palace."

His wife urged him to do the same, and so, the Butterfly stamped again. The Djinns restored the palace and the gardens to their original place. The nine hundred and ninety-nine Queens ran out of the palace screaming and calling out for their babies. Balkis told them what had happened but they didn't believe her.

"Our Palace cannot be plucked for the sake of a little insect," an Egyptian Queen exclaimed. "Suleiman-bin-Daoud must be dead! That was an omen."

Balkis led the other Queens to the King, who had a butterfly on each hand.

"Remember to please your husband," Suleiman-bin-Daoud said to the Butterfly's wife. "He is a great magician to steal the Palace of Suleiman-bin-Daoud himself."

Then, he kissed them both on their wings, and they flew away.

If a Butterfly can cause this by being displeased with his wife, then what will happen to us who have irritated our King, the Queens thought. They put their veils on, covered their mouths with their hands, and quietly tip-toed back to the Palace.

"Rejoice, my Lord," Balkis stated to Suleiman-bin-Daoud. "We have taught the Queens of Egypt, Persia, Ethiopia, China, India, and Abyssinia a great and memorable lesson."

Then, she told her husband what she had done.

"If I had made a Magic against my Queens in pride or anger, I would have certainly been shamed just like I was at the feast for all animals," Suleiman-bin-Daoud said, as he rejoiced. "But thanks to your wisdom, I made the Magic in jest and for a little butterfly, and it has delivered me from the irritations of my wives. How did you become so wise, My Lady?"

Balkis the Most Beautiful looked into Suleiman-bin-Daoud's eyes and replied, "Firstly, because I loved you; and secondly, because I know what women are like!"

Then, they lived happily ever after. But wasn't Balkis a clever lady?

About the Author

■ Rudyard Kipling

Rudyard Kipling was born on 30 December 1865 in Bombay, India. When he was six years old, Kipling was sent to England to study. As he struggled in his new surroundings, he derived solace in books and reading, and was inspired by the works of Daniel Defoe, Ralph Waldo Emerson and Wilkie Collins.

In 1882, Kipling returned to India as a journalist, writing fiction in his spare time. He returned to England in 1889 as a popular and established writer. Rudyard Kipling was awarded the Nobel Prize for Literature in 1907.

Although Kipling's 'The Jungle Books' and 'Captains Courageous' are regarded as his best works, 'Just So Stories' is also among his best-known works. Originally published as 'The Just So Stories for Little Children', Kipling composed these delightful tales as bedtime stories for his daughter Josephine, who tragically died of pneumonia in 1899. Kipling named this collection after Josephine's phrase 'just so', used by Josephine, asking her father to repeat the stories exactly as they were.

■ Questions

Chapter 1

- 1. *Why were there no more fish left in the sea? Who was the only one who survived and how?*
- 2. *How did the Mariner escape from the whale's belly? Explain in detail.*

Chapter 2

- 1. *Who were the Three? Why were they angry with the Camel?*
- 2. *How did the Djinn make the lazy Camel work? Explain in detail.*

Chapter 3

- 1. *Why was the Parsee angry with the Rhinoceros?*
- 2. *How did the Parsee extract his revenge?*

Chapter 4

- 1. *Who were the two hunters in the High Veldt Area? Describe them in detail.*
- 2. *How did the other animals fool the Leopard and the Ethiopian?*

Chapter 5

- 1. *Why was the Elephant's Child spanked? Who spanked him?*
- 2. *How did the Elephant's Child get his trunk?*

Chapter 6

- 1. *Who were the Gods that the Kangaroo visited and why? What was the outcome of these visits?*
- 2. *Why did the Dingo chase the Kangaroo? What happened at the end of the chase?*

Chapter 7

- *1. What advice did the Mother Jaguar give to Painted Jaguar?*
- *2. How did the clever Hedgehog and the Tortoise fool Painted Jaguar?*

Chapter 8

- *1. Who was the stranger? What did Taffy tell him to do?*
- *2. Describe what happened immediately after the stranger found Taffy's mother.*

Chapter 9

- *1. Who was responsible for the invention of the first alphabet? Taffy or Tegumai? Explain with reasons.*
- *2. What did Taffy and his father do after creating the alphabet? How long did this task take them?*

Chapter 10

- *1. Who was Pau Amma? Why did he not follow the instructions of the Eldest Magician?*
- *2. How did the Eldest Magician bring Pau Amma under control?*

Chapter 11

- *1. Describe how the Woman tamed the first wild animal.*
- *2. What was the bargain that the Man and the Dog made with the Cat? Explain.*

Chapter 12

- *1. Why was Suleiman-bin-Daoud sad? Explain.*
- *2. Who was Balkis? How did she help Suleiman-bin-Daoud get back his peace of mind?*